GREEN LANTERN

For Green Lanterns Only

screenplay by Greg Berlanti & Michael Green &
Marc Guggenheim and Michael Goldberg, screenstory by Greg
Berlanti & Michael Green & Marc Guggenheim, based upon
characters appearing in comic books published by DC Comics.

PSS!

PRICE STERN SLOAN
An Imprint of Penguin Group (USA) Inc.

PRICE STERN SLOAN
Published by the Penguin Group
Penguin Group (USA) Inc., 375 Hudson Street, New York, New York 10014, USA
Penguin Group (Canada), 90 Eglinton Avenue East, Suite 700, Toronto, Ontario M4P 2Y3, Canada
(a division of Pearson Penguin Canada Inc.)
Penguin Books Ltd., 80 Strand, London WC2R 0RL, England
Penguin Group Ireland, 25 St. Stephen's Green, Dublin 2, Ireland (a division of Penguin Books Ltd.)
Penguin Group (Australia), 250 Camberwell Road, Camberwell, Victoria 3124, Australia
(a division of Pearson Australia Group Pty. Ltd.)
Penguin Books India Pvt. Ltd., 11 Community Centre, Panchsheel Park, New Delhi—110 017, India
Penguin Group (NZ), 67 Apollo Drive, Rosedale, Auckland 0632, New Zealand
(a division of Pearson New Zealand Ltd.)
Penguin Books (South Africa) (Pty.) Ltd., 24 Sturdee Avenue, Rosebank, Johannesburg 2196, South Africa

Penguin Books Ltd., Registered Offices: 80 Strand, London WC2R 0RL, England

The publisher does not have any control over and does not assume any responsibility
for author or third-party websites or their content.

ISBN 978-0-8431-9840-9   10 9 8 7 6 5 4 3 2 1

Access to the
following top secret
information is
restricted to members
of the Green Lantern
Corps only.

All unauthorized
access is strictly
prohibited.

BIO

HAL JORDAN IS A FORMER TEST PILOT. HE WAS CHOSEN TO BE THE FIRST GREEN LANTERN FROM EARTH BECAUSE OF HIS COURAGE AND ABILITY TO OVERCOME FEAR.

DATA

REAL NAME: HAL JORDAN

OCCUPATION: GREEN LANTERN/GALACTIC PROTECTOR/PILOT

BASE OF OPERATIONS: SECTOR 2814

HOMEWORLD: EARTH

HEIGHT: 6' 2"

WEIGHT: 186 LB.

EYES: BROWN

HAIR: BROWN

ATTRIBUTES

GREEN LANTERN POWER RING

EXPERT FIGHTER PILOT

FEARLESSNESS AND STRONG WILL

FIRM MORAL CODE

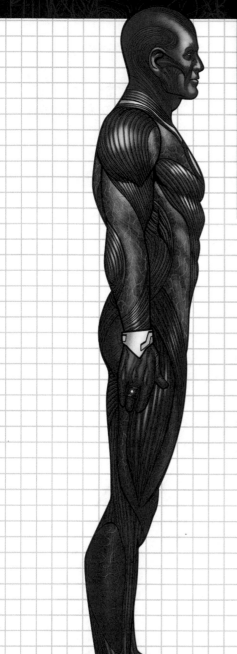

BIO

ABIN SUR IS ONE OF THE GREATEST GREEN LANTERNS OF ALL TIME. AFTER HE CRASH-LANDED ON EARTH, HIS POWER RING CHOSE HAL JORDAN TO REPLACE HIM IN THE GREEN LANTERN CORPS.

DATA

REAL NAME: ABIN SUR

OCCUPATION: GREEN LANTERN/ GALACTIC PROTECTOR

BASE OF OPERATIONS: SECTOR 2814

HOMEWORLD: UNGARA

HEIGHT: 6'1"

WEIGHT: 200 LB.

EYES: BLUE

HAIR: NONE

ATTRIBUTES

GREEN LANTERN POWER RING

RECOGNIZED HERO OF THE GREEN LANTERN CORPS

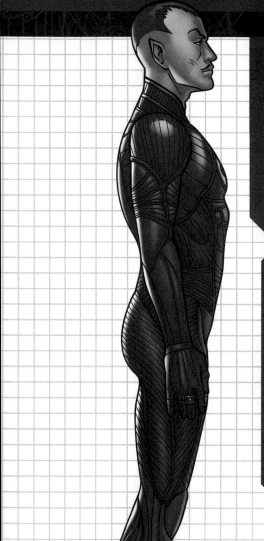

BIO

SINESTRO IS CONSIDERED BY MANY TO BE THE GREATEST GREEN LANTERN IN THE CORPS. HE IS ONE OF THE LEADERS OF THE GREEN LANTERN CORPS.

DATA

REAL NAME: THAAL SINESTRO

OCCUPATION: GREEN LANTERN/ GALACTIC PROTECTOR

BASE OF OPERATIONS: SECTOR 1417

HOMEWORLD: KORUGAR

HEIGHT: 6'7"

WEIGHT: 204 LB.

EYES: BLACK

HAIR: BLACK

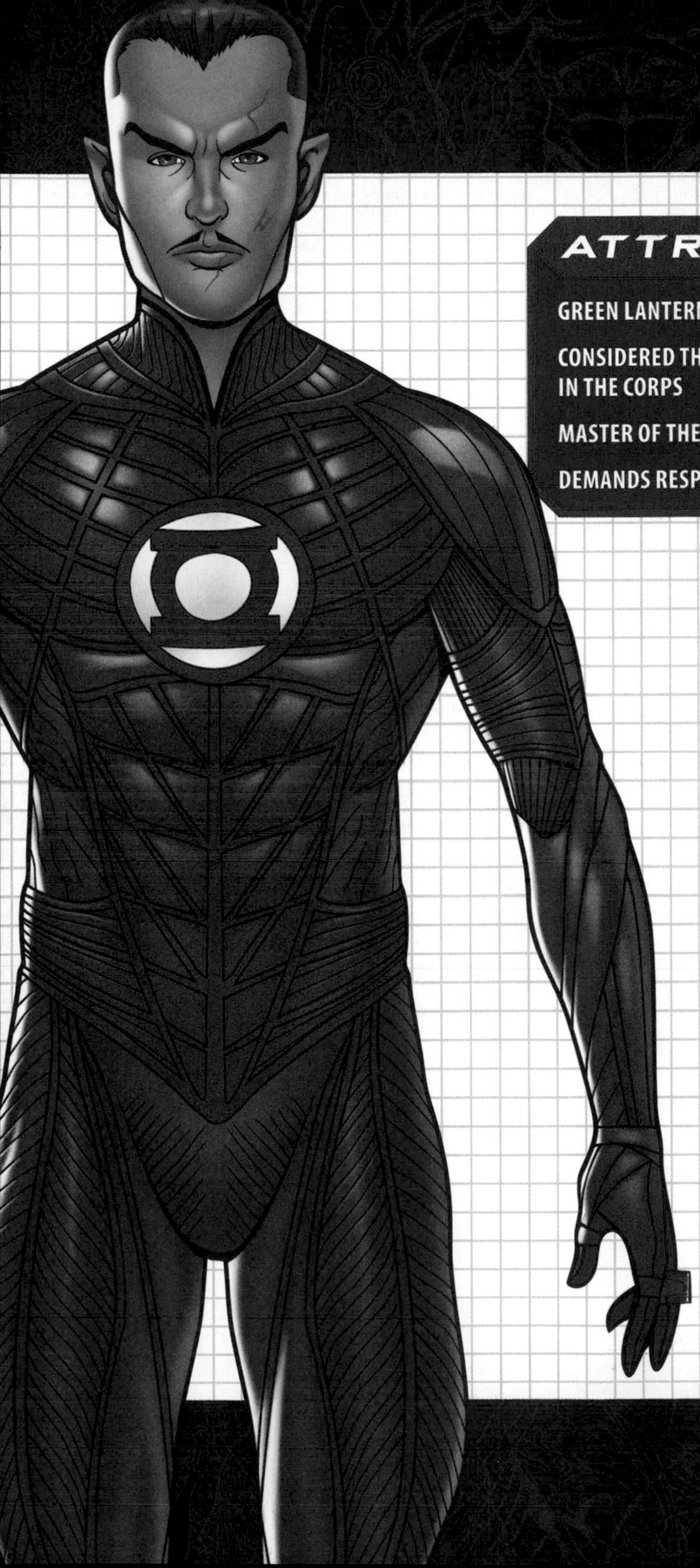

ATTRIBUTES

- GREEN LANTERN POWER RING
- CONSIDERED THE BEST GREEN LANTERN IN THE CORPS
- MASTER OF THE POWER RING
- DEMANDS RESPECT FROM HIS PEERS

BIO

KILOWOG IS A POWERFUL MEMBER OF THE GREEN LANTERN CORPS. HIS JOB IS TO TRAIN THE NEW RECRUITS WHEN THEY ARRIVE ON OA.

DATA

REAL NAME: KILOWOG

OCCUPATION: GREEN LANTERN/GALACTIC PROTECTOR/DRILL INSTRUCTOR/GENETICIST

BASE OF OPERATIONS: SECTOR 674

HOMEWORLD: BOLOVAX VIK

HEIGHT: 8' 0"

WEIGHT: 720 LB.

EYES: RED

HAIR: NONE

ATTRIBUTES

GREEN LANTERN POWER RING

SUPERIOR STRENGTH AND IMPRESSIVE FORCE

MASTER INSTRUCTOR ON USING POWER RING

TOMAR-RE

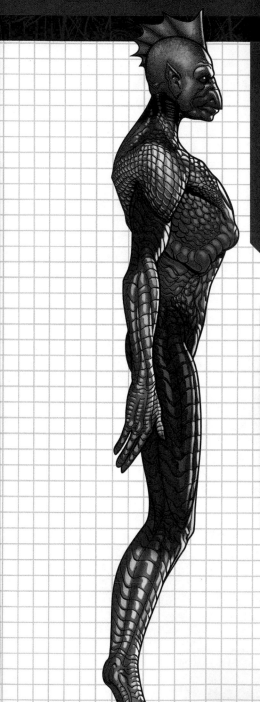

BIO

TOMAR-RE'S CURIOSITY HAS LED HIM TO STUDY THE SACRED BOOK OF OA AT GREAT LENGTH. THE GUARDIANS OF THE UNIVERSE HAVE APPOINTED HIM PROTECTOR OF THE BOOK.

DATA

REAL NAME: TOMAR-RE

OCCUPATION: GREEN LANTERN/GALACTIC PROTECTOR/ARCHIVIST

BASE OF OPERATIONS: SECTOR 2813

HOMEWORLD: XUDAR

HEIGHT: 7' 0"

WEIGHT: 220 LB.

EYES: RED

HAIR: NONE

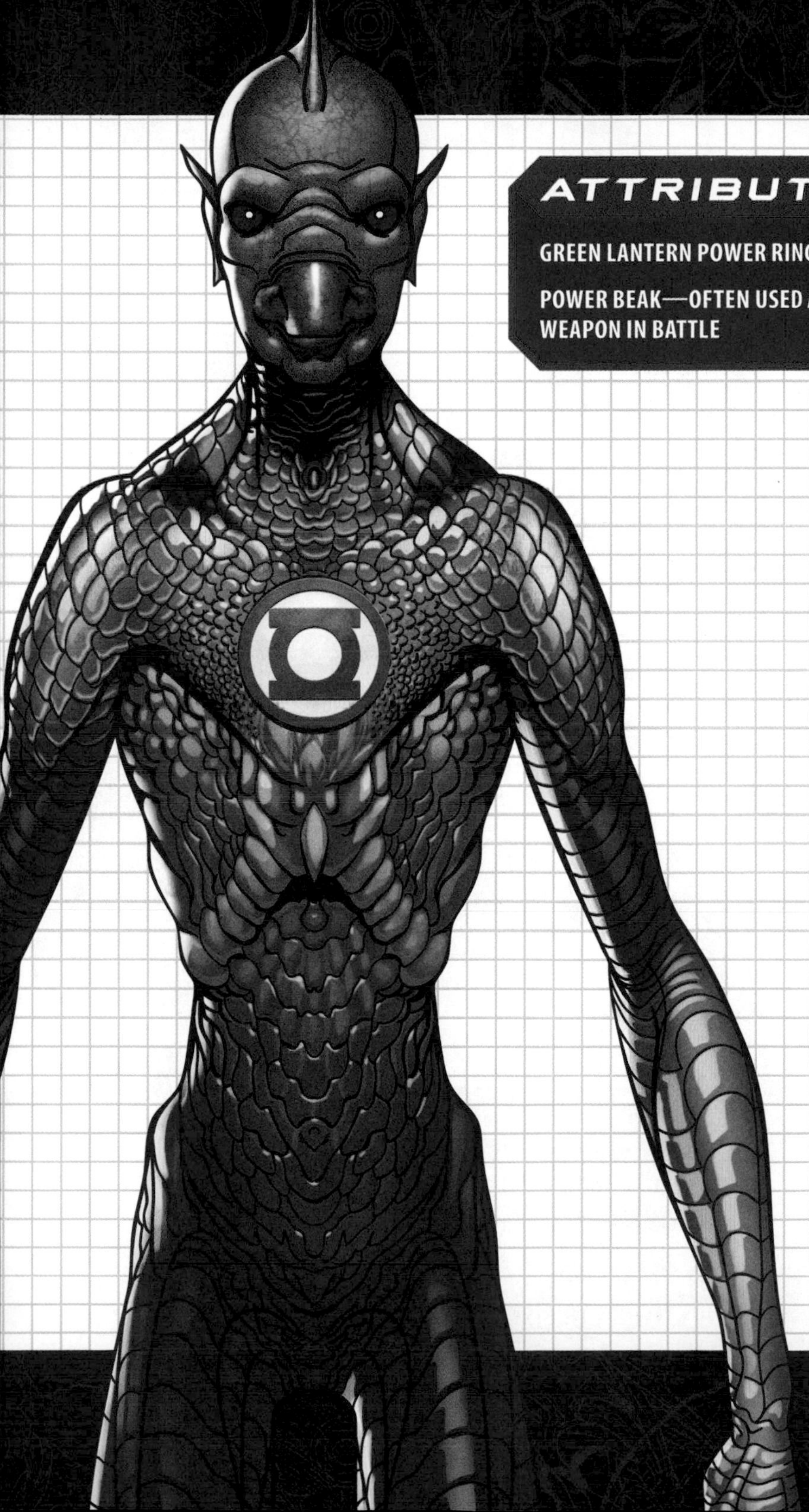

ATTRIBUTES

GREEN LANTERN POWER RING

POWER BEAK—OFTEN USED AS A WEAPON IN BATTLE

BIO

SAYD IS A MEMBER OF THE GUARDIANS OF THE UNIVERSE. RELATIVELY YOUNG FOR A GUARDIAN, SHE IS THE VOICE FOR PROGRESS WITHIN THE COUNCIL RANKS.

DATA

REAL NAME: SAYD

OCCUPATION: GUARDIAN OF THE UNIVERSE

BASE OF OPERATIONS: PLANET OA, SECTOR 0000

HOMEWORLD: MALTUS

HEIGHT: 3'5"

WEIGHT: 75 LB.

EYES: BLUE

HAIR: NONE

ATTRIBUTES

NEAR IMMORTALITY

ABLE TO MANIPULATE WILLPOWER ENERGY WITHOUT A RING

SUPERIOR INTELLIGENCE

TELEPATHY—ABLE TO SPEAK WITH OTHER LIVING BEINGS

FLIGHT

BIO

GANTHET IS A FOUNDING MEMBER OF THE GUARDIANS OF THE UNIVERSE. HE INSTRUCTS THE GREEN LANTERNS IN BRINGING PEACE THROUGHOUT THE UNIVERSE.

DATA

REAL NAME: GANTHET

OCCUPATION: GUARDIAN OF THE UNIVERSE

BASE OF OPERATIONS: PLANET OA, SECTOR 0000

HOMEWORLD: MALTUS

HEIGHT: 3'5"

WEIGHT: 135 LB.

EYES: GREEN

HAIR: WHITE

ATTRIBUTES

NEAR IMMORTALITY

ABLE TO MANIPULATE WILLPOWER ENERGY WITHOUT A RING

SUPERIOR INTELLIGENCE

TELEPATHY—ABLE TO SPEAK WITH OTHER LIVING BEINGS

FLIGHT

BIO

BARIS IS A MEMBER OF THE GUARDIANS OF THE UNIVERSE. SHE POSSESSES TREMENDOUS INTELLIGENCE AND MIGHT BE AMONG THE MOST GIFTED OF ALL THE GUARDIANS.

DATA

REAL NAME: BARIS

OCCUPATION: GUARDIAN OF THE UNIVERSE

BASE OF OPERATIONS: PLANET OA, SECTOR 0000

HOMEWORLD: MALTUS

HEIGHT: 3'6"

WEIGHT: 78 LB.

EYES: GRAY

HAIR: NONE

ATTRIBUTES

NEAR IMMORTALITY

ABLE TO MANIPULATE WILLPOWER ENERGY WITHOUT A RING

SUPERIOR INTELLIGENCE

TELEPATHY—ABLE TO SPEAK WITH OTHER LIVING BEINGS

FLIGHT

BIO

HERUPA IS A MALTUSIAN AND MEMBER OF THE GUARDIANS OF THE UNIVERSE. HE HAS LITTLE TOLERANCE FOR CHANGE OR THE OPINIONS OF THE GREEN LANTERNS.

DATA

REAL NAME: HERUPA

OCCUPATION: GUARDIAN OF THE UNIVERSE

BASE OF OPERATIONS: PLANET OA, SECTOR 0000

HOMEWORLD: MALTUS

HEIGHT: 3'9"

WEIGHT: 89 LB.

EYES: VIOLET

HAIR: NONE

ATTRIBUTES

NEAR IMMORTALITY

ABLE TO MANIPULATE WILLPOWER ENERGY WITHOUT A RING

SUPERIOR INTELLIGENCE

TELEPATHY—ABLE TO SPEAK WITH OTHER LIVING BEINGS

FLIGHT

BIO

AMANITA IS A FUNGUS LIFE-FORM FROM THE SWAMP-WORLD PLANET OF MUSCARIA. HE HAS ACHIEVED A HIGHER CONSCIOUSNESS OVER HIS EXTREMELY LONG LIFE SPAN.

DATA

REAL NAME: AMANITA

OCCUPATION: GREEN LANTERN/GALACTIC PROTECTOR/ARTIST

BASE OF OPERATIONS: SECTOR 3100

HOMEWORLD: MUSCARIA

HEIGHT: 4'0"

WEIGHT: 48 LB.

EYES: BROWN

HAIR: NONE

ATTRIBUTES

GREEN LANTERN POWER RING

AN UNCANNY COSMIC CONSCIOUSNESS

INCREDIBLE LIFE SPAN

ARTIST

APROS

BIO

APROS IS ONE OF THE OLDEST MEMBERS OF THE CORPS AND HIS UNUSUAL PLANTLIKE APPEARANCE MAKES HIM STAND APART FROM THE OTHERS.

DATA

REAL NAME: APROS

OCCUPATION: GREEN LANTERN/FORMER HONOR GUARD/GREEN LANTERN TRAINER

BASE OF OPERATIONS: SECTOR 3

HOMEWORLD: 7PI

HEIGHT: 8'5"

WEIGHT: 340 LB.

EYES: NONE

HAIR: NONE

ATTRIBUTES

GREEN LANTERN POWER RING

PSIONIC ABILITIES—ABLE TO IDENTIFY WEAKNESS IN ANOTHER BEING

POWERFUL MIND—RECOGNIZED FOR HIS POTENT RING CREATIONS

BOODIKKA

BIO

BOODIKKA COMES FROM A WARRIOR RACE ON THE ROUGH TERRAIN OF BELLATRIX. HER TALENTS USING A POWER RING HAVE MADE HER ONE OF THE CORPS'S FIERCEST MEMBERS.

DATA

REAL NAME: BOODIKKA

OCCUPATION: GREEN LANTERN/ WARRIOR/MERCENARY

BASE OF OPERATIONS: SECTOR 1414

HOMEWORLD: BELLATRIX

HEIGHT: 6' 10"

WEIGHT: 125 LB.

EYES: GREEN

HAIR: BLACK

ATTRIBUTES

GREEN LANTERN POWER RING

MASTER AT HAND-TO-HAND COMBAT

AGGRESSIVE NATURE

BZZD

BIO

BZZD IS AN INSECTILE FROM THE PLANET APIATON. WHILE SMALL IN SIZE, BZZD IS WELL RESPECTED BY HIS PEERS BECAUSE OF HIS TREMENDOUS WILLPOWER.

DATA

REAL NAME: BZZD

OCCUPATION: GREEN LANTERN

BASE OF OPERATIONS: SECTOR 2261

HOMEWORLD: APIATON

HEIGHT: 1'3"

WEIGHT: 6 LB.

EYES: RED

HAIR: NONE

ATTRIBUTES

GREEN LANTERN POWER RING

OMNI-DIRECTIONAL VISION

SUPER-SPEED

VENOMOUS STINGER

BIO

BORN ON THE PLANET BARRIO III, CHASELON IS A CRYSTALLINE LIFE-FORM. HE IS EXTREMELY DURABLE AND HAS LIVED A LONG LIFE.

DATA

REAL NAME: CHASELON

OCCUPATION: GREEN LANTERN

BASE OF OPERATIONS: SECTOR 12

HOMEWORLD: BARRIO III

HEIGHT: 4'11"

WEIGHT: UNKNOWN

EYES: UNKNOWN

HAIR: NONE

ATTRIBUTES

GREEN LANTERN POWER RING

POSSESSES THIRTEEN SENSES—HAS PERCEPTIONS FAR BEYOND THOSE OF HUMANS

EXTREMELY DURABLE

COMMUNICATES THROUGH UNIVERSAL HARMONICS—TONES RECOGNIZED BY ALL LIVING LIFE-FORMS

BIO

ALWAYS READY FOR A FIGHT, GALIUS ZED DELIGHTS IN CHARGING INTO BATTLE WITH AN OVERSIZED CRANIUM THAT FORMS THE BULK OF HIS BODY.

DATA

REAL NAME: GALIUS ZED

OCCUPATION: GREEN LANTERN/ GALACTIC PROTECTOR

BASE OF OPERATIONS: SECTOR 1123

HOMEWORLD: NOC'SAG

HEIGHT: 5'2"

WEIGHT: 1,265 LB.

EYES: BLACK

HAIR: NONE

ATTRIBUTES

GREEN LANTERN POWER RING

TREMENDOUS STRENGTH

G'HU

BIO

G'HU IS A HUMANOID FROM THE PRISON-PLANET TAKRON-GALTOS. HIS UNIQUE PHYSICAL FEATURES AND DEXTERITY IN THE FIELD MAKE HIM AN UNPREDICTABLE OPPONENT.

DATA

REAL NAME: G'HU

OCCUPATION: GREEN LANTERN/ PRISON GUARD

BASE OF OPERATIONS: SECTOR 2937

HOMEWORLD: UNKNOWN

HEIGHT: 7'0"

WEIGHT: 260 LB.

EYES: GREEN

HAIR: NONE

ATTRIBUTES

GREEN LANTERN POWER RING

SHARP TALONS

POWERFUL "BRAID-TAILS"—CAPABLE OF SPEARING HIS ATTACKERS

GREEN MAN

BIO

BORN ON THE WORLD OF UXOR, GREEN MAN QUICKLY PROVED HIS FIGHTING PROWESS AND EARNED HIS PLACE AS AN ELITE MEMBER OF THE GREEN LANTERN CORPS.

DATA

REAL NAME: N/A (MEMBERS OF HIS RACE HAVE NO INDIVIDUALITY)

OCCUPATION: GREEN LANTERN/ GALACTIC PROTECTOR

BASE OF OPERATIONS: SECTOR 2828

HOMEWORLD: UXOR

HEIGHT: 6′4″

WEIGHT: 210 LB.

EYES: RED

HAIR: NONE

ATTRIBUTES

GREEN LANTERN POWER RING

TELEPATHY CAPABILITIES

AMPHIBIOUS

BLOOD CONTAINS DEADLY NERVE TOXIN

BIO

HANNU IS A MASSIVE HUMANOID WITH FLESH THAT RESEMBLES STONE. HIS WARRIOR INSTINCTS OFTEN GRAVITATE MORE TOWARD BRUTE STRENGTH THAN RELIANCE ON HIS RING.

DATA

REAL NAME: HANNU

OCCUPATION: GREEN LANTERN

BASE OF OPERATIONS: SECTOR 2

HOMEWORLD: OVACRON 6

HEIGHT: 10'0"

WEIGHT: 720 LB.

EYES: WHITE

HAIR: NONE

ATTRIBUTES

GREEN LANTERN POWER RING

TREMENDOUS STRENGTH

MASTER AT HAND-TO-HAND COMBAT

DAMAGE-RESISTANT—DENSE PHYSICAL FORM

BIO

ISAMOT KOL IS A REPTILIAN HUMANOID. NOTORIOUS FOR HIS CUNNING AND WILL TO SURVIVE, ISAMOT IS A BATTLE-TESTED WARRIOR.

DATA

REAL NAME: ISAMOT KOL

OCCUPATION: GREEN LANTERN/ GALACTIC PROTECTOR

BASE OF OPERATIONS: SECTOR 2682

HOMEWORLD: THANAGAR

HEIGHT: 4' 6"

WEIGHT: 193 LB.

EYES: YELLOW

HAIR: NONE

ATTRIBUTES

GREEN LANTERN POWER RING

POWERFUL JAW AND SHARP TEETH

LIGHTNING-FAST TAIL

BIO

LARVOX ORIGINATES FROM THE PLANET SPUTAN, A WORLD WHERE INSECTS AND PLANTS ARE THE MAIN SPECIES. LARVOX COMMUNICATES BY USING HIS POWER RING.

DATA

REAL NAME: LARVOX

OCCUPATION: GREEN LANTERN/ GALACTIC PROTECTOR

BASE OF OPERATIONS: SECTOR 17

HOMEWORLD: SPUTAN

HEIGHT: 5'6"

WEIGHT: 230 LB.

EYES: BROWN (ONE EYE)

HAIR: ORANGE

ATTRIBUTES

GREEN LANTERN POWER RING

FIERCE BATTLE SKILLS

BIO

LIN CANAR IS A CREATURE OF PLANT MATTER. AS A MEMBER OF HIS PLANET'S SCIENTIFIC TEAM, LIN CANAR POSSESSES AN ANALYTIC MIND AND AN EXPLORER'S CURIOSITY.

DATA

REAL NAME: LIN CANAR

OCCUPATION: GREEN LANTERN/ OCEANOGRAPHER

BASE OF OPERATIONS: SECTOR 1582

HOMEWORLD: FLUVIAN

HEIGHT: 8'9"

WEIGHT: 100 LB.

EYES: GREEN

HAIR: NONE

ATTRIBUTES

GREEN LANTERN POWER RING

EXPERT SWIMMER—ABLE TO WITHSTAND INTENSE PRESSURE

VISIBILITY IN LOW-LIGHT CONDITIONS

EXCEPTIONAL STRENGTH UNDERWATER

BIO

ONE OF THE ONLY KNOWN SURVIVORS OF THE LOST WORLD OF ZANNER, M'DAHNA FOUND HIS PLACE IN THE GREEN LANTERN CORPS AFTER SHOWING HIS REMARKABLE WILLPOWER.

DATA

REAL NAME: M'DAHNA

OCCUPATION: GREEN LANTERN/ GALACTIC PROTECTOR

BASE OF OPERATIONS: SECTOR 2751

HOMEWORLD: ZANNER

HEIGHT: 7'2"

WEIGHT: 320 LB.

EYES: LIGHT BROWN (ONE EYE)

HAIR: NONE

ATTRIBUTES

GREEN LANTERN POWER RING

UNWAVERING COMMITMENT TO THE GREEN LANTERN CORPS

BIO

MEDPHYLL IS A SENTIENT PLANT LIFE-FORM. HE POSSESSES A SPECIAL ABILITY TO EXCHANGE THOUGHTS WITH OTHER FLORA.

DATA

REAL NAME: MEDPHYLL

OCCUPATION: GREEN LANTERN/ GALACTIC PROTECTOR

BASE OF OPERATIONS: SECTOR 586

HOMEWORLD: J586

HEIGHT: 5'0"

WEIGHT: 68 LB.

EYES: BLACK (ONE EYE)

HAIR: N/A (MIND STALKS)

ATTRIBUTES

GREEN LANTERN POWER RING

ABLE TO COMMUNICATE WITH OTHER PLANT LIFE

BIO

LEARNING TO SURVIVE ON THE HARSH DESERT WORLD OF SARC, MORRO HONED HIS FIGHTING SKILLS IN AN UNFORGIVABLE LANDSCAPE.

DATA

REAL NAME: MORRO

OCCUPATION: GREEN LANTERN/ CRYPT KEEPER

BASE OF OPERATIONS: SECTOR 666

HOMEWORLD: SARC

HEIGHT: 5'7"

WEIGHT: UNKNOWN

EYES: BLACK

HAIR: NONE

ATTRIBUTES

GREEN LANTERN POWER RING

PET DRATURES—DRAGON-LIKE BEASTS THAT PROTECT THE GREEN LANTERN CRYPT

SOLITARY, PREFERS ISOLATION

BIO

NAUT KE LOI IS AN AQUATIC BEING FROM THE PLANET AEROS. HE ALWAYS WEARS A WATER-FILLED HELMET TO KEEP HIM ALIVE.

DATA

REAL NAME: NAUT KE LOI

OCCUPATION: GREEN LANTERN/ GALACTIC PROTECTOR

BASE OF OPERATIONS: SECTOR 12

HOMEWORLD: AEROS

HEIGHT: 5'0"

WEIGHT: 305 LB.

EYES: YELLOW

HAIR: NONE

ATTRIBUTES

GREEN LANTERN POWER RING

BREATHES UNDERWATER

RAZOR-SHARP HEAD FINS

AGILE SWIMMER

SCALES EXUDE DEADLY SECRETION

BIO

A RECENT RECRUIT TO THE GREEN LANTERN CORPS, NGILA G'RNT IS BLESSED WITH THE BOUNDLESS SPARK OF YOUTH AND A STRONG DESIRE TO DEMONSTRATE HER TALENTS.

DATA

REAL NAME: NGILA G'RNT

OCCUPATION: GREEN LANTERN

BASE OF OPERATIONS: SECTOR 542

HOMEWORLD: INGUANZO

HEIGHT: 5'6"

WEIGHT: 100 LB.

EYES: VIOLET

HAIR: NONE

ATTRIBUTES

GREEN LANTERN POWER RING

IMPRESSIVE AGILITY IN MOST ENVIRONMENTS

EXTRAORDINARY SENSE OF HEARING

NORCHAVIUS

BIO

A RECRUIT FROM THE FLOATING ISLANDS OF GRA'VAR, NORCHAVIUS IS RENOWNED FOR PROJECTING CONSTRUCTS OF GREAT BEAUTY WHILE FIGHTING HIS ENEMIES.

DATA

REAL NAME: NORCHAVIUS

OCCUPATION: GREEN LANTERN/ GALACTIC PROTECTOR/SCULPTOR

BASE OF OPERATIONS: SECTOR 26

HOMEWORLD: GRA'VAR

HEIGHT: 7' 6"

WEIGHT: 63 LB.

EYES: YELLOW

HAIR: NONE

ATTRIBUTES

GREEN LANTERN POWER RING

RECOGNIZED FOR HIS ARTISTIC RING EMISSIONS

POWERFUL TAIL

SHARP BEAK

HAWK-LIKE EYES OFFER SUPERIOR VISION

BIO

PENELOPS IS AN AQUATIC BEING FROM THE OCEAN PLANET PENELO, A PLACE WHERE ITS UNDERWATER INHABITANTS FEAR LIGHT AND LIVE IN DARKNESS BENEATH THE WAVES.

DATA

REAL NAME: PENELOPS

OCCUPATION: GREEN LANTERN/ GALACTIC PROTECTOR

BASE OF OPERATIONS: SECTOR 3155

HOMEWORLD: PENELO

HEIGHT: 5'6"

WEIGHT: 268 LB.

EYES: BLUE (ONE EYE)

HAIR: NONE

ATTRIBUTES

GREEN LANTERN POWER RING

TENTACLES WITH ELECTRIC SHOCK

INK PROJECTIONS TO BLIND ATTACKERS

KEEN EYESIGHT IN LOW-LIGHT TERRAINS

CAMOUFLAGE CAPABILITIES IN WATER

BIO

BORN THE PRINCESS OF A RULING FAMILY ON THE WAR-TORN WORLD OF BETRASSUS, IOLANDE WAS SELECTED OVER HER BROTHERS TO JOIN THE RANKS OF THE GREEN LANTERN CORPS.

DATA

REAL NAME: IOLANDE

OCCUPATION: GREEN LANTERN/ PRINCESS OF BETRASSUS

BASE OF OPERATIONS: SECTOR 1417

HOMEWORLD: BETRASSUS

HEIGHT: 6'4"

WEIGHT: 120 LB.

EYES: PURPLE

HAIR: NONE

ATTRIBUTES

GREEN LANTERN POWER RING

PHOTOGRAPHIC MEMORY

BIO

R'AMEY HOLL SERVED AS A LAW OFFICER ON HER HOME PLANET OF PAPILLIOX. SHE WAS BORN WITH MAJESTIC WINGS WHICH ALLOW HER TO FLY EVEN WITHOUT HER POWER RING.

DATA

REAL NAME: R'AMEY HOLL

OCCUPATION: GREEN LANTERN/ GALACTIC PROTECTOR

BASE OF OPERATIONS: SECTOR 700

HOMEWORLD: PAPILLIOX

HEIGHT: 4'6"

WEIGHT: 114 LB.

EYES: ORANGE

HAIR: BROWN

ATTRIBUTES

GREEN LANTERN POWER RING

BUTTERFLY WINGS

ANTENNAE CAN SENSE HER SURROUNDINGS

BIO

HAILING FROM THE OBSIDIAN DEEPS, ROT LOP FAN IS A SILICON-BASED LIFE-FORM THAT IS COMPLETELY BLIND TO THE VISIBLE SPECTRUM.

DATA

REAL NAME: ROT LOP FAN

OCCUPATION: GREEN LANTERN/ GALACTIC PROTECTOR

BASE OF OPERATIONS: SECTOR 911

HOMEWORLD: OBSIDIAN DEEPS

HEIGHT: 6'0"

WEIGHT: 230 LB.

EYES: N/A (BLIND)

HAIR: N/A (SILICON)

ATTRIBUTES

GREEN LANTERN POWER RING

EXTRAORDINARY HEARING

SILICON FORM IS HEAT/LIGHT RESISTANT

RELIES ON MUSICAL F-SHARP BELL TO CREATE RING CONSTRUCTS

BIO

RESIDING AT GREEN LANTERN HEADQUARTERS IN SECTOR ZERO, SALAAK SERVES AS THE HEAD TACTICIAN AND CENTRAL OPERATIONS FOR THE GUARDIANS OF THE UNIVERSE.

DATA

REAL NAME: SALAAK

OCCUPATION: GREEN LANTERN/ GALACTIC PROTECTOR

BASE OF OPERATIONS: SECTOR 1418, REASSIGNED TO SECTOR 0

HOMEWORLD: SLYGGIA

HEIGHT: 7' 6"

WEIGHT: 207 LB.

EYES: WHITE

HAIR: NONE

ATTRIBUTES

GREEN LANTERN POWER RING

OVERSEES OPERATIONS FOR THE GUARDIANS OF THE UNIVERSE

HIGHLY ADEPT AT MULTI-TASKING

BIO

VOZ COMES FROM THE HOSTILE WORLD OF ECIRAM, ONE OF THE DEADLIEST PLACES IN THE GALAXY. HE SERVES AS THE WARDEN OF THE SCIENCELLS, THE MOST SECURE PRISON IN THE COSMOS.

DATA

REAL NAME: VOZ

OCCUPATION: GREEN LANTERN/ GALACTIC PROTECTOR/WARDEN

BASE OF OPERATIONS: SECTOR 571

HOMEWORLD: ECIRAM

HEIGHT: 8'0"

WEIGHT: 816 LB.

EYES: BROWN

HAIR: BROWN (FUR)

ATTRIBUTES

GREEN LANTERN POWER RING

SHARP CLAWS ON HANDS AND FEET

ACUTE SENSE OF SMELL

TREMENDOUS STRENGTH

BIO

THE PLANET OA IS HOME TO THE GUARDIANS OF THE UNIVERSE AND THE HEADQUARTERS OF THE GREEN LANTERN CORPS. THE GUARDIANS PICKED OA, ONCE A BARREN AND LIFELESS WORLD, FOR ITS LOCATION AT THE CENTER OF THE COSMOS. ALSO REFERRED TO AS SECTOR ZERO, OA PROVIDES GREEN LANTERNS A PLACE TO GATHER, TRAIN, AND DISCOVER MORE ABOUT THE UNIVERSE THEY SERVE AND PROTECT.

DATA

REAL NAME: OA

FUNCTION: HEADQUARTERS OF THE GREEN LANTERN CORPS

BASE OF OPERATIONS: SECTOR 0

ATTRIBUTES

HEADQUARTERS OF THE GREEN LANTERN CORPS

LOCATION OF THE CENTRAL POWER BATTERY

FEARLESS AND STRONG WILL

SECTOR ZERO—CENTER OF THE KNOWN UNIVERSE

BIO

ABIN SUR DESIGNED HIS SPACECRAFT FOR UTILITY MORE THAN COMFORT, WHICH REFLECTS HIS OWN PRACTICAL NATURE. ALTHOUGH GREEN LANTERNS DO NOT REQUIRE SPACE VEHICLES FOR TRAVEL ACROSS THE COSMOS, ABIN SUR HAD GOOD REASON TO KEEP HIS POWER RING AT MAXIMUM CHARGE, JUST IN CASE HE WAS FACED WITH ANY UNFORESEEN CRISES.

DATA

CLASS: TRANSPORT VEHICLE

BASE OF OPERATIONS: SECTOR 2814

HOMEWORLD: UNGARA

HEIGHT: 40'

WEIGHT: 48,000 LB.

ATTRIBUTES

CAPABLE OF TRAVELING FASTER THAN LIGHT

HEAVILY SHIELDED

STOCKED WITH ESCAPE PODS, SURVIVAL GEAR, FOOD AND WATER

AMPLE CARGO SPACE FOR TRANSPORT OF SUPPLIES OR PRISONERS

COMPATIBLE WITH POWER RING CONSTRUCTS

BIO

USED FOR A VARIETY OF MENIAL TASKS ON OA, THIS UNMANNED UTILITY SPACECRAFT IS DESIGNED TO DO ANYTHING FROM REPAIRING A BUILDING TO MANAGING GROUNDS KEEPING. PILOTED VIA TELEPATHY OR PREPROGRAMMED OPERATIONS, IT IS EQUIPPED WITH A NUMBER OF APPENDAGES, RANGING FROM A HEAVY-DUTY CRANE ARM TO FINE TENDRILS FOR DELICATE WORK.

DATA

CLASS: UTILITY CRAFT

BASE OF OPERATIONS: PLANET OA, SECTOR 0000

HOMEWORLD: OA

HEIGHT: 194'

WEIGHT: UNKNOWN

ATTRIBUTES

INNER-ATMOSPHERIC TRAVEL AT SUB-LIGHT SPEEDS

MINIMAL SHIELDING AND NO WEAPONRY

MULTIPLE UTILITY ATTACHMENTS

PILOTED BY TELEPATHY OR PREPROGRAMMED

BIO

THE EQUIVALENT OF OAN "BUSES," THESE POD-LIKE CRAFTS CAN CARRY UP TO SEVERAL HUNDRED LIFE-FORMS AT RELATIVELY HIGH SPEEDS TO ANY POINT ON THE PLANET OA.

DATA

CLASS: TRANSPORT CRAFT

BASE OF OPERATIONS: PLANET OA, SECTOR 0000

HOMEWORLD: OA

HEIGHT: 110'

WEIGHT: UNKNOWN

ATTRIBUTES

INNER-ATMOSPHERIC TRAVEL AT SUB-LIGHT SPEEDS

MINIMAL SHIELDING AND NO WEAPONRY

PILOTED BY TELEPATHY OR PREPROGRAMMED

BIO

THE POWER BATTERY, OR "LANTERN," IS THE RECHARGING UNIT FOR EACH GREEN LANTERN'S POWER RING. THE BATTERY TAPS INTO THE ENERGY OF THE CENTRAL POWER BATTERY ON PLANET OA AND SERVES AS A PORTABLE CONNECTION. ANY MEMBER OF THE CORPS CAN SUMMON THEIR POWER BATTERY AT WILL AND MUST ALWAYS RECITE THE SACRED GREEN LANTERN OATH WHEN RECHARGING THEIR RINGS: *IN BRIGHTEST DAY, IN BLACKEST NIGHT, NO EVIL SHALL ESCAPE MY SIGHT. LET THOSE WHO WORSHIP EVIL'S MIGHT BEWARE MY POWER . . . GREEN LANTERN'S LIGHT!*

DATA

REAL NAME: GREEN LANTERN PERSONAL POWER BATTERY

HEIGHT: 1'2"

WEIGHT: 1 LB. 4 OZ.

ATTRIBUTES

CHANNELS POWER DIRECTLY FROM THE CENTRAL POWER BATTERY ON THE PLANET OA

CAN BE SUMMONED INSTANTANEOUSLY

BIO

BUILT ON THE PLANET OA BY THE GUARDIANS OF THE UNIVERSE, THE CENTRAL POWER BATTERY IS A RESERVOIR OF ENERGY FOR THE GREEN LANTERN CORPS. CHARGED WITH THE COMBINED WILLPOWER OF EVERY SENTIENT BEING IN THE GALAXY, THE BATTERY EMITS ENERGY TO THE MEMBERS OF THE GREEN LANTERN CORPS WHO POSSESS INDIVIDUAL POWER RINGS.

DATA

REAL NAME: GREEN LANTERN CENTRAL POWER BATTERY

FUNCTION: EMPOWERS GREEN LANTERN CORPS

BASE OF OPERATIONS: SECTOR 0

HEIGHT: 300'

HOMEWORLD: OA

ATTRIBUTES

STORES THE EMOTIONAL ENERGY OF WILLPOWER

POWER RING

BIO

FORGED WITHIN THE OAN FOUNDRY BY THE GUARDIANS OF THE UNIVERSE, POWER RINGS GIVE GREEN LANTERNS THE ABILITY TO CREATE ENERGY CONSTRUCTS FROM THEIR OWN IMAGINATIONS. ONLY THOSE WHO DEMONSTRATE THE STRENGTH OF WILLPOWER ARE ABLE TO WIELD THE RINGS. THE STRONGER THE WILL, THE MORE EFFECTIVE THE RING BECOMES.

ATTRIBUTES

CAPABLE OF CREATING ANYTHING THE USER IMAGINES

POWER LIMITED ONLY BY THE USER'S IMAGINATION

MUST BE CHARGED EVERY TWENTY-FOUR EARTH HOURS

DATA

REAL NAME: GREEN LANTERN POWER RING

HOMEWORLD: FOUNDRY ON OA

HEIGHT: 1.2"(AVERAGE)

WEIGHT: 5 OZ.